Weather

El tiempo

el tee-*empo*

Illustrated by Clare Beaton

Ilustraciones de Clare Beaton

BARRON'S

rain

la lluvia

lah *yoo*-beeah

sun

el sol

el sol

fog

la niebla

lah nee-*eh*blah

snow

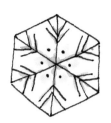

la nieve

lah nee-*ehveh*

ice

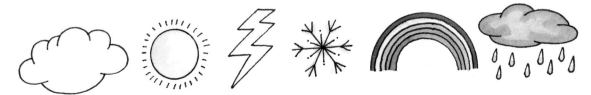

el hielo

el *yeh*lo

wind

el viento

el bee-*en*to

cloud

la nube

lah *noobeh*

thunder

el trueno

el troo*weh*-no

lightning

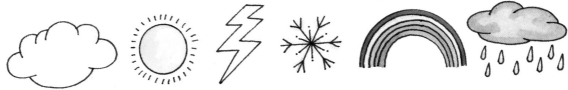

el relámpago

el rel–*la*mpah–go

storm

la tormenta

lah tor-*mentah*

rainbow

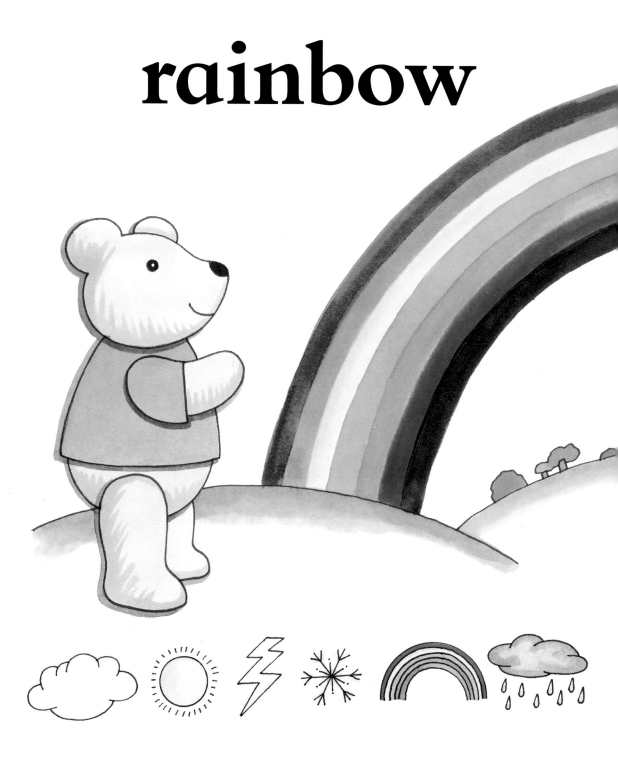

el arco iris

el arko *eeriss*

A simple guide to pronouncing the Spanish words

- Read this guide as naturally as possible, as if it were English.
- Put stress on the letters in *italics,* for example, lah *yoo*-beeah.

la lluvia	lah *yoo*-beeah	**rain**
el sol	el sol	**sun**
la niebla	lah nee-*eh*blah	**fog**
la nieve	lah nee-*eh*veh	**snow**
el hielo	el *yeh*lo	**ice**
el viento	el bee-*en*to	**wind**
la nube	lah *noo*beh	**cloud**
el trueno	el troo*weh*-no	**thunder**
el relámpago	el rel-*lam*pah-go	**lightning**
la tormenta	lah tor-*men*tah	**storm**
el arco iris	el arko *eer*iss	**rainbow**

Text and illustrations © Copyright 2001 b small publishing, Surrey, England
First edition for the United States, Canada, and the Philippines published 2001 by Barron's Educational Series, Inc.
All rights reserved. No part of this book may be reproduced in any form, by photostat, microfilm, xerography, or any other means, or incorporated into any information retrieval system, electronic or mechanical, without the written permission of the copyright owner.
Address all inquiries to: Barron's Educational Series, Inc., 250 Wireless Boulevard, Hauppauge, New York 11788
http://www.barronseduc.com
ISBN-13: 978-0-7641-1690-2,   ISBN-10: 0-7641-1690-8
Library of Congress Catalog Card Number 00-110627
Printed in China   987